THIS LEVINSON BOOK
BELONGS TO:

_____

_____

First published in 1997 in Great Britain by
Levinson Children's Books,
Winchester House, 259-269 Old Marylebone Road,
London, NW1 5XJ.

10 9 8 7 6 5 4 3 2

Text © Ian Whybrow 1997
Illustrations © Adrian Reynolds 1997

The right of Ian Whybrow and Adrian Reynolds to be identified
as the author and illustrator of this work has been asserted by them
in accordance with the Copyright Designs and Patent Act 1988.

ISBN 1-899607-85-4 hardback
ISBN 1-86233-032-8 paperback

A CIP record for this title is available from the British Library.

Printed and bound in Italy

Harry and the Snow King

By Ian Whybrow

Illustrated by Adrian Reynolds

LEVINSON BOOKS

for Suzannah & Lucy
I. W.

for Giovanna
A. R.

When the snow came, you had to look for it.
But Harry had waited long enough.
He went out with his spoon and plate.

He put out his tongue and caught a flake.
It was just right.

There was some in the corner by the woodpile.
There was a good bit by the henhouse.

And if you were very careful
you could scoop it off the leaves.

It took all morning to find enough snow
to make the snow king.

Nan called, "What are you doing out there?"
"Nothing," he said. But he was looking
on the holly for red buttons.

Mum called, "Are you hungry?"
"Not yet," he said.
He was hungry, but he was making a crown.

Sam said, "Your soup is cold, stupid."
"Coming," he said, and brought the
snow king to show them.

They all bowed down to look.

Sam said not to bring him in,
it was too warm inside.

That was why Harry left
   the snow king on the wall.

He ate his soup and told about the snow king.

Sam said big snowmen were better and he was stupid not to have waited.

That was why Harry threw his bread at Sam.

Nan took him to his room
to settle down.

Later, the snow king was not on the wall.

"You just give him back!" Harry said.
But Sam had been watching TV all the time.

The snow king was
nowhere in the yard.
He was not in the refrigerator.

"Somebody kidnapped him," said Harry.

He wanted to call the police
but Mum said better not to bother them.

Four o'clock, Mr Oakley passed
on his tractor. Harry said
about his snow king
being kidnapped.

Mr Oakley looked up at the sky.
He said not to give up hope.
He said maybe the snow king
went to order more snow.

Next morning there were
snowpeople all over the yard.

Ten at least. Wonderful!
And white everywhere, everywhere you looked!

Mr Oakley drove by on his way back from milking. "I found these earlier," he said. He opened his hand to show the red buttons and the crown.

"I hoped all night," said Harry.
"I never gave up. It was just like you said.
The snow king went to order some more snow,
but he left me these snowpeople."

"Hitch up your sledge," said Mr Oakley.
"This looks like good snow for getting towed
by a tractor. Shall we go now, or wait for Sam?"

"Sam's watching TV," said Harry.

"We'll come back for her later then,"
  said Mr Oakley. "You get first go."

Harry and Sam had a lot of fun that day.
But, that first go was just
the best.